Dinosaurs Explore!

Adapted by May Nakamura
Based on the television series created by Craig Bartlett

SIMON SPOTLIGHT
New York London Toronto Sydney New Delhi

Here is a list of all the words you will find in this book. Sound them out before you begin reading the story.

Names:

Dinosaurs

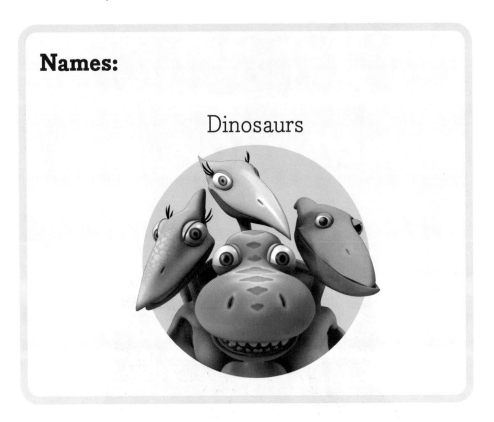

SIMON SPOTLIGHT

An imprint of Simon & Schuster Children's Publishing Division · 1230 Avenue of the Americas, New York, New York 10020 · This Simon Spotlight edition May 2019

For information about special discounts for bulk purchases, please contact Simon & Schuster Special Sales at 1-866-506-1949 or business@simonandschuster.com. Manufactured in the United States of America 0419 LAK
1 2 3 4 5 6 7 8 9 10 · ISBN 978-1-5344-3038-9 (hc) · ISBN 978-1-5344-3037-2 (pbk) · ISBN 978-1-5344-3039-6 (eBook)

Word families:

"-ig" →	big	dig
"-ound" →	ground	round
"-ore" →	more	explore

Sight words:

a	all	are	do
find	go	into	is
like	play	ride	some
the	these	they	this
to	under	what	will

Bonus words:

cave	friend	friends	rocks	train

Ready to go? Happy reading!

Don't miss the questions about the story
on the last page of this book.

The dinosaurs ride the train.

The train will go into a cave.

The cave is under the ground.

The dinosaurs dig.
The dinosaurs explore.

What do they find?

They find big rocks.
The rocks are round.

The dinosaurs
explore some more.

The dinosaurs
find a friend!

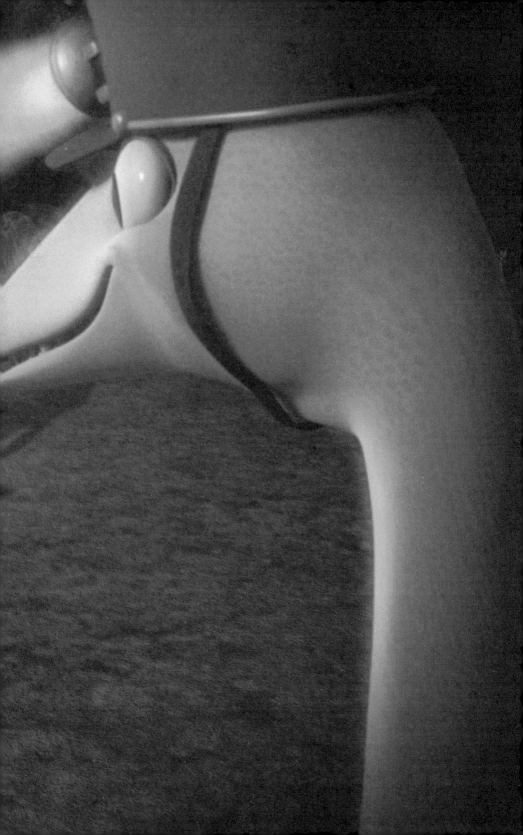

The dinosaurs explore some more.

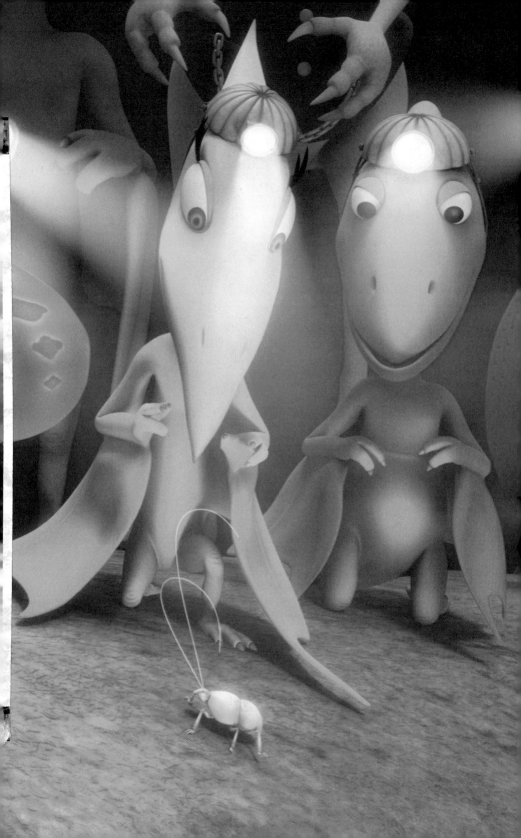

The dinosaurs
find more friends!

They all play.

GROWN-UPS, READ THESE PAGES WITH YOUR CHILD IF THEY'D LIKE TO LEARN MORE ABOUT THE EARTH.

Bonus information about the Earth's layers!

Did you know that the Earth is made up of different layers? The crust is the top layer of the Earth. This is where dinosaurs lived (and where humans live too!). The mantle is the second layer. The outer core and the inner core are the deepest layers of the Earth.

Now that you have read the story, can you answer these questions?

1. Where is the cave?

2. What are some of the things that the dinosaurs find in the cave?

3. In this story, you read the rhyming words "more" and "explore." Can you think of other words that rhyme with "more" and "explore"?

Great job!
You are a reading star!